Tidying Up

It's tidy-up time.

E

By Jani   enceley

Co   wood

CHERRYTREE BOOKS

A CHERRYTREE BOOK

This edition first published in 2007
by Cherrytree Books, part of
The Evans Publishing Group Limited
2a Portman Mansions
Chiltern Street
London W1U 6NR

Printed in China

British Library Cataloguing in Publication Data

Amos, Janine
 Being helpful. - Rev. ed. - (Growing up)
 1. Helping behaviour - Pictorial works - Juvenile literature
 I. Title
 302.1'4

ISBN 9781842344934

CREDITS
Editor: Louise John
Designer: D.R.ink
Photography: Gareth Boden
Production: Jenny Mulvanny

Based on the original edition of Being Helpful published in 1997

With thanks to: Gareth Boden, Aman Jutla, Samuel Mark, Emma and Abi Coomber, Lauren Griffiths.

"Let's put everything back. Then we'll be able to find it tomorrow," says Gareth.

Sam puts the bricks
back in the box.

Aman puts the
dough in the tub.

Aman finds a brick in the dough.
He takes it to Sam.

Sam has packed all
the bricks away.

Aman is still busy.
What could Sam do?

Sam goes over to Aman.
"I can help you now," he says.

They clear up the rest
of the dough together.

"We've finished!" says Sam.

"You worked together," says Gareth. "You helped each other."

Helping Mum

"Waah!" Abi is crying.

"She's been crying all night!"
sighs Mum.

"Do you want your rattle, Abi?" asks Mum.

"Nah!" says Abi.

"Do you want your drink, Abi?"
asks Mum.

"Nah!" says Abi.

"Brrr!" goes
the telephone.
"Waah!"
cries Abi.

22

"Oh, no!" sighs Mum.
How does Mum feel?

Lauren goes over to Abi.

She makes a funny face.

Abi smiles.

Lauren wiggles her fingers.

Abi laughs.

Lauren laughs too. "She's happy now," says Lauren.

"Thanks, Lauren,"
smiles Mum.

"You helped Abi –
and that helped me."

Teachers' Notes

The following extension activities will assist teachers in delivering aspects of the PSHE and Citizenship Framework as well as aspects of the Healthy Schools criteria.

Specific areas supported are:

- Framework for PSHE&C 1b, 1c, 1e, 2a, 2e, 2h, 4a, 4b, 4d, 5b, 5f
- National Healthy School Criteria 1.1, 4.3

Activity for *Tidying Up*

Read the story to the children.

- Ask them to think about all the ways we can work together, identifying tasks and situations in which helping one another is important.
- Set up a display board with a cut-out paper vase labelled 'We have been helping each other'.
- Every time a group of children co-operate in working together, playing together or completing a task together, add a flower to the vase. Use a circle of paper for the centre with the activity written/drawn on it. Then write the names of the children who have helped each other on the petals. Some flowers will be like chrysanthemums with almost every name in the class on, others like tulips with two large overlapping petals and others like daisies with half a dozen petals. Draw the children's attention to each new flower as it is completed and talk about the actions behind it.

Activity for *Helping Mum*

Read the story to the children.

- Sit the children in a circle with a flipchart at child height.
- Remind the children about the answers they gave to the question posed in the text on p23 about Mum's feelings.
- Ask the children:
  Does their mum ever feel like this?
  How do they know this is how she is feeling?
  How does it show?
- Ask the children to work in pairs around the circle. Each child has to tell their partner something they can do to help their mum when she is feeling like Mum in the story.
- When all the children have thought of something, go round the circle and ask each child to share their idea. These can be written up or drawn onto the flipchart. Label the list 'Things we can do to help Mum'.
- Tell the children that for one week they are to try and think of something they can do to help Mum every day.
- Every morning for the next week ask who has done something to help and invite some of the children to tell the class what they did. If there are new ways of helping mentioned, these can be added to the list.
- Each day hang a new length of string under the list. Ask every child who has been helpful to Mum to thread a large bead onto the string so that as a class they can see how many helpful things have been done each day. Label each string with the day of the week and hang them all side by side to compare length.